# THE TYRANNOSAURUS TIC

## A BOY'S ADVENTURE WITH TOURETTE SYNDROME

### "Pre-Diagnosis"

## STEPHEN MICHAEL MCCALL

### Illustrated by: Nea Zambrana

Order this book online at www.trafford.com
or email orders@trafford.com

Most Trafford titles are also available at major online book retailers.

Note for Librarians: A cataloguing record for this book is available from Library
and Archives Canada at www.collectionscanada.ca/amicus/index-e.html

Printed in the United States of America.

ISBN: 978-1-4251-5501-8 (sc)

*Trafford rev. 05/11/2011*

 www.trafford.com

**North America & international**
toll-free: 1 888 232 4444 (USA & Canada)
phone: 250 383 6864 ♦ fax: 250 383 6804 ♦ email: info@trafford.com

# THE TYRANNOSAURUS TIC

A BOY'S ADVENTURE WITH TOURETTE
SYNDROME
"Pre-Diagnosis"

A part of the:

Tyrannosaurus Tic Series

*This book is dedicated to my mom, Marilyn Penn Scott a.k.a. "Mrs. Connie," and my Aunt Brenda for always encouraging me that I could be something in life even with a disorder.*

*Miguel*

# CONTENTS

# PREFACE

TOURETTE SYNDROME (TS) is a neurological disorder that many times is misunderstood by the media. Oftentimes, TS is known as the cursing disease, which is inaccurate. In actuality, this is a very rare piece of TS with only about 10% of individuals having TS showing signs of "coprolalia." Even with that, the person does not randomly scream vulgar words at people the way movies have portrayed.

People with TS are very intelligent and many live normal lives. There are doctors, lawyers, preachers, teachers, actors, military veterans, professional sports players, and many more who have TS and have overcome the challenges and beat the odds.

For children with TS, it is very difficult to understand what is going on with their bodies when they make involuntary movements, called "tics," both motor and vocal. However, there are ways to suppress these movements. It takes patience and time to learn how to suppress them. It is not always easy but possible.

This is the first book of the *Tyrannosaurus Tic* series, which gives the account of a boy named Michael living in the pre-diagnosis stages of Tourette Syndrome. The next book is a continuation of Part One leading up to the diagnosis and how he learns to overcome the challenges (post-diagnosis). It is written from the point of view of a pre-adolescent child and how he perceives what is going on in his body. How a 12-year-old views things is quite different from an adult. The story is based on true experiences and situations; however, some of the ways he views things are quite funny. The book presents his challenges. Be prepared to laugh, cry, and really feel with the main character.

Remember every story involving people with TS is not negative, and many of those stories have happy endings. Though there are obstacles one must overcome, you will see how Michael chose to overcome his! Enjoy.

# ACKNOWLEDGEMENTS

T HE FOLLOWING people were contributors in making this book possible and my dream of publishing it come true! I thank the following people and all of those who had faith in me!

Tyrannosaurus Tic Series
Acknowledgements
The following have made this
book possible with their generous
donations
6/1/2008
Stephen Michael McCall

### *Editing, Ideas, and Suggestions on Design:*

Dr. Crystal Lucky, Mr. Victor Lawrence, Mr. Kevin Nether, Ms. Janie McClurkin, Ms. Nea Zambrana, Ms. Melissa McCall, Mr. Larry Cayenne McCall

### *TSA Acknowledgements:*

Mrs. Judit Ungar (President of TSA), Ms. Tracy Colletti-Flynn (Public Relations of TSA), Mrs. Sue Jacobs (Executive Director, TSAGW), Mrs. Jessica Gibson (Co-Leader of Tidewater TSA Support Group), Khristopher Gibson (My mentor and role model)

### *Personal Acknowledgements:*

Dr. Joseph White, Bishop T.L. Lucky, C.L.G.I. executive board, Elder Charles and Min Yasmine Robinson, Dr. Eric & Dr. Christiana Russell, Mr. James & Luv Johnson, Mr. Nick & Kennita Williams, Mr. Randy & Vanita Brunson

## *MAJOR Contributors*
(under $50):

Mr. Chris Ladezma; Mr. and Mrs. Durward Sr., Mary Jane, Durward Jr.,Titus, and Micah Till; Ms. Marilyn Penn Scott; Danny, Jessica, Heaven, and Khristopher Gibson; Mr. and Mrs. Kim & Carol Chisolm and children, Kimmel & Kimmaya; Mrs. Pamela Hendricks; Mr. and Mrs. Jameela White

## *DISTINGUISHED Contributors*
($50-$99):

Mr. and Mrs. Ernest & Kenya Bracey and children; Mr. and Mrs. Alex & Kim Agyemang and twins Adam and Kai; Ms. Amber Cooke

## *MINOR TIC SPONSOR*
($100-$199):

Ms. Monica Alegria; Joshua Ladezma; Mr. Kere & Brenda Cawley

## *TYRANNOSAURUS TIC SPONSOR*
($200 & above):

Ms. Patricia Dickerson; Mr. and Mrs. Steven & Janine Wiggins, and son Phillip; Autism Association of Maryland

# 1

---

# IN THE BEGINNING: "SIMPLE TICS"

HI, MY name is Michael, and I'm 12 years old. This is an exciting time for me because tomorrow is June 10th and it's my birthday. Yes, and you figured it out. I finally become a teenager. All of my friends are coming over for my birthday party and we are going to have fun. As I sit back and think over the past two years of my life, it has been a roller coaster! If you would have told me that this day would be exciting for me back then, I would have laughed and said, "NEVER!"

The first year was one of the hardest. My body started doing things out of my control, from twitching to making different noises. In the beginning, I was getting in trouble at home and at school because everyone thought I was being a big clown, but in my mind I thought, "Duh, I haven't gone to clown college yet. I'm too young."

To my parents' surprise, there was a reason for my weird behavior. I was recently diagnosed with a disorder I call Tyrannosaurus Rex Syndrome [Tourette Syndrome]. I really don't understand how I was infected with a dinosaur's disorder, but I promise I did not touch the dinosaur exhibits at the science museum. Okay, maybe I did, but hey, I am a curious kid. What do you expect? It all started when I was 10 years old.

"Ring! Ring! Ring!" the alarm sounded as I woke up hearing my mother in the near distance.

"Michael, wake up!" Mom said. "It's time to get up. Michael, wake up!"

I rubbed my eyes in hopes that it was a dream. I finally rolled out of my bed and slipped my feet into the cold slippers to start yet another ordinary day of school. My eyes began to blink quickly while I walked to the bathroom to brush my teeth. I accidentally ran into my older brother, Larry.

"Michael, what are you doing?" Larry said. "Get off me before I tell mom."

Larry is 17 years old. I think it's illegal in Michigan, where we live, for him to treat kids my age, especially little brothers, with any respect. That's why I plan to move to another state before my 17th birthday so I don't get arrested for treating people nice.

I looked into the bathroom mirror and tried to stop blinking my eyes so much. I figured that playing my Play Station 2 (PS2) so much the night before had messed with my eyes. My mom always tells me that playing too many video games will turn a kid into a video game. I don't think this is accurate information because my brother would have been a game boy a long time ago. Then I figured that I didn't get enough sleep.

While I brushed my teeth, my eyes kept blinking like there was a mosquito stuck under my eye lid. I couldn't figure out what was happening to me. My eyes had been doing this for over a month and it was getting worse.

After I got dressed, I ran down the stairs to grab some breakfast.

"Mom, Michael is running down the stairs again!" Larry screamed.

"What in the world is wrong with this dude?" I thought. "Is my brother's goal in life to get me in trouble?"

I sat down at the kitchen table to eat my favorite cereal, Fruity Pebbles.

"Stop blinking your eyes so much, Michael." Mom said. "Haven't I told you over and over?"

"I can't stop!" I said sadly. "My eyes are taking over my body."

You can guess what she said next.

"Michael, I told you that playing video games too much will make your eyes blink uncontrollably. Now you can't stop."

"Mom, you told me that I would turn into a

video game," I said in shock.

"Okay, that's true, but first comes the blinking eyes."

Now, I'm not a rocket scientist, but my mom works at a bank downtown. I don't remember her telling me she went to school to be a video game doctor. Of course, I didn't tell her that. Then my eyes would really be blinking!

I kissed my mom goodbye and ran out of the house. I had an eye appointment that day and hoped it would be during reading class so I wouldn't have to read in front of the class. You can only guess how hard it's been for me to read without getting stares and laughs from my classmates. Since my eyes have been acting up, the kids at school sort of notice it, duh.

# 2

---

## THE WORLD RECORD FOR EYE TWITCHING

"WHAT'S UP, Mike?" my friend Curt said on the way to the bus stop.

"I get to go to the eye doctor today," I said. "Tomorrow I won't blink anymore."

On the school bus, everyone looked like zombies. They had the opposite problem from me. Their eyes didn't blink at all. They just sat there staring and then falling asleep. I don't understand why adults make kids get up at 6 o'clock in the morning for school. They don't start work until 8. Being a kid is hard. At least in Michigan it is. We don't get out of school until 3 o'clock, and then we have to do homework! There has to be another state with easier rules and no homework. If you know of one, please let me know, so I can move.

My eyes were doing their own thing as I sat on the bus. It was frustrating. Every time I tried to make them stop, it seemed as if they said, "No, and if you ask us again, we're going to blink even harder."

Before I got to school, I let my eyes do whatever they wanted. Then when we got to school, I tried my best not to blink. But if I didn't blink for a few minutes, it got worse. I just couldn't win.

The big yellow bus came to a halt, and all of the kids woke up from their morning naps. Finally, we have arrived to school. From the time I woke up that morning, it had been around an hour and a half. I should have called the Guinness Book of World Records, because I set a record for the world's fastest and most consecutive blinks on a bus ride. I must have blinked 10 billion catrillion times. I'm not sure if catrillion is a real number, but my brother always tells me that in a catrillion years, he's going to let me come in his room. So I know it's a BIG number.

I fumbled with my book bag and let everyone get off the bus before me. I had made this a habit because once I got off the bus, kids start noticing my blinking. You see, I have to outsmart everyone else to keep from being embarrassed. I have a list of excuses for why I blink.

## MICHAEL'S LIST OF EXCUSES #1

1. I have allergies even though it's not allergy season.

2. I'm doing a science project on goldfish that have blinking problems.

3. I'm practicing for the Olympics in "Eye Blinking."

4. I have super powers in my eyes that allow me to see through walls, and it causes me to blink fast.

5. I'm not blinking. What are you talking about?

Most of my excuses don't work, but I still try to use the top 3, hoping someone will believe me and stop asking questions. I just hoped that it was going to be a good day with no questions. Now that's funny. A day without questions, impossible!

# 3

# A DOG IN THE CLASSROOM

"RING! RING! Ring!" the five-minute bell sounded.

I only had four minutes left to hang with my friends before the tardy bell rang. First period that day was Science with Mrs. Brunson. We were presenting our topics for the Science Fair. I hoped my mom would come to pick me up because I didn't know if I could hold my eyes down.

I walked into the classroom and right away I became a target.

"Good Morning, Michael," Mrs. Brunson said. "I don't want a comedy show out of you this morning as you give your science project."

"Great," I thought to myself, starting to sweat in fear. I walked to my desk and felt the urge to blink and blink and blink and blink and ….oops. Mrs. Brunson didn't understand that the more pressure I had, the worse my eyes blinked. I didn't know how I was going to get out of the presentation. I felt like the whole world was against me.

Kathleen, one of my best friends from second grade, stood up and did her presentation. Her science project was on her dog, Cookiemon. During her speech, there was a loud bark-like sound.

"What in the world is going on?" I thought as the kids looked around the room trying to figure out where the bark was coming from.

I looked around and then realized it was me. Why did I make that noise? No one realized it was me, but I knew I was a suspect. My heart started to beat very fast as my name was called next.

"Mr. Michael, it is your turn," Mrs. Brunson said.

I walked up to the front of the class. I heard kids laughing and snickering in back of me. They were ready for a show. Mrs. Brunson stared me down with a look in her eyes.

"You better not act up," she said, "or I'm going to send you to the Principal's office."

I turned around and walked to the front of the class. My eyes were blinking worse than ever before.

"Hello, my name is Michael." I said to begin my speech. "My presentation is on BARK!

EEEeeeP! Eeeep!"

The kids fell on the floor laughing as I shouted out these weird sounds.

"Eeeeep, BARK, RUF, Eeeep!" I screamed again.

"Meet me in the hallway, Michael." Mrs. Brunson said.

I knew I was doomed. All of the kids in my class were still laughing until tears came out of their eyes. I walked out of the class, and the kids cheered and clapped.

"Way to go Mike," one kid said. "Make some more animal voices."

"Hey Mike, Ruf Ruf, Ruf," another kid said, laughing.

The more they made fun of me, the more tears came to my eyes. Since my eyes were blinking more than normal, of course I could not hold the tears from falling down my face.

"Michael, I don't know what I'm going to do with you," Mrs. Brunson said in frustration. "Why do you insist on disobeying me and trying to make everyone laugh with your outbursts?"

I looked at Mrs. Brunson and thought it would be a good time to give one of my famous excuses. Do you think I did it? What did I have to lose? Choose from the list below. If you guess right, you'll win the grand prize.

MICHAEL'S LIST OF EXCUSES #2

1. I have allergies even though it's not allergy season. (This excuse works for any situation, so it's on all of my lists.)

2. I work for the Dogs of America Association and am required to bark at least 35 times a day.

3. I am practicing for a play called, "All Dogs Bark in Ticville."

4. That wasn't a bark. That was a scream. So what's the problem?

Which excuse do you think I chose? If you guessed number 1, 2, 3, or 4, you're wrong.

Thanks for playing! Okay, that wasn't fair. So I'll give you the grand prize anyway since I'm nice. You win the chance to read the rest of the book! Ha! Ha!

"Mrs. Brunson, you see what happened was, this morning when I was eating some cookies," I stuttered, "I realized I was accidentally eating my dog's biscuits. Now, it's making me turn into a dog."

Oh no! Did I actually just say that? I don't even have a dog. She's going to think I'm an idiot. What was I thinking?

"Michael, that is enough," Mrs. Brunson said. "I'm taking you to the principal's office."

I couldn't believe that I was going to have to explain this to my principal. What was I going to say? No one believed me when I said that I couldn't help the eye twitches. So how was I going to explain the barks?

I walked down the hallway, feeling as if I couldn't hold back my eyes ticcing. And now, to add to the drama, I had this new tic, the bark. I was so embarrassed. I held it in the best I could and went into the principal's office and sat down. I waited until they called my mom to pick me up. I felt a little better because my mom was on her way to pick me up and rescue me from being held hostage. Okay, maybe I'm taking it too far, but I felt like I was in jail. I sat there thinking of reasons why this was happening to me. Why did I have to be the only kid in the world with an eye twitch and a dog bark? I felt like the entire world was against me. I didn't ever want to come back to school! People were always looking at me, and my teachers had labeled me as a trouble maker. All I could think was "Why me?"

My mother finally arrived. She immediately went into my principal's office for a meeting with the teacher. I knew that couldn't be good. They closed the door while I waited outside in the office area. I sat there trying to think of what punishment I was going to get. Maybe it would only be for a year. I hope it wasn't the video games. Ahhhhhhh!!!!!! My life was over!

The suspense was killing me. The door remained closed and I waited to see what was going to happen. I knew my principal was making me look like the world's worst kid. Finally, I saw the principal's door open slowly, and there was my mother shaking the enemy's, I mean, the principal's hand. She told me to grab my bag so we could go home. She didn't say a word to me, but I could tell she was holding back tears. I didn't want to disappoint my mom, but I didn't know what else to do. Until someone, anyone, could tell me why my body was acting the way it was, there was nothing I could do to change it. I fell asleep as soon as I sat down in the car, hoping when we arrived at the eye doctor, my tics would be completely gone.

That evening at the dinner table, I found out that my eyes were perfectly normal. So why in the world were my eyes twitching? After dinner, my mom sat down next to me on the couch and acted like nothing was wrong with my new and improved barking outbursts. I was expecting a long speech about the dangers of barking in class, but to my surprise, she didn't say a word.

"So Michael, do you want to play a board game?" mom asked.

"Am I daydreaming?" I thought amazed. "Or is my mom actually going crazy?"

But as the night went on, I realized my mom was on my side. She acted like nothing was wrong with me at all! I have the world's greatest mom! Sorry, but she's not for sale. She is all mine!

# 4

## THE ROBOTIC HANDS

"THERE IS a snow storm warning today for the Detroit Metropolitan Area," the weatherman said on the TV. "We expect to get around 8-12 inches of snow."

I was so excited. I decided to take my school clothes off and get ready to go back to sleep.

"All public schools are open. Classes are not cancelled."

What! Were they crazy? It was a blizzard outside and they wanted us to die in the snow? Because I was upset, this "creature" in my body woke up. Whenever I get excited or sad, my tics act up more. So, I try to stay calm and relaxed at all times. However, when I told my mother it would be best for me to drop out of school and play video games all day to keep me relaxed, she said no. At least I tried.

Outside, the clouds looked dark and puffy, but the snow was barely falling. I wished the weatherman would change his mind and make it snow harder. If I were him, I would have made it snow so they would shut down the weather station. But no, he wanted to stay on the air and torture me. I put my shoes on, but my hands started to move like the hands on a robot. My fingers started to expand and go in all sorts of ways. I tried to tie my shoes again, but it was very hard because of the urge to stretch my hands and fingers. I wondered why my hands were going crazy. I thought that maybe I had played too many video games and that had caused my hands to turn into remote controls.

"Put your shoes on, Michael," Larry said. "And stop messing with your hands or I'm telling Dad."

I looked at him and barked a few times to be funny. I didn't have an urge to bark, but since I'd been barking for the past couple of months, I figured it would be cool to bark at him since I wouldn't get in trouble. But if Larry called my Dad, that would be another story. My brother is very smart. He knows just who to call in any situation. When he wants to get me in trouble for twitching, he calls my father. When it comes to my playing soccer in the living room, he calls my mom.

My father came downstairs and asked me what the problem was. Of course, I told him nothing. I finally got my shoes on and held back my hand from twitching. It felt like my hands were going to fall off. It was almost impossible for me to control it. I used all of my strength and ... mission accomplished! I got my shoes on just in time to run to the bus stop and wondered what adventures were going to happen that day.

Every day is an adventure in my life. The biggest adventure was going to school because people looked at me funny, expecting me to act up. It had become somewhat of a problem. I used to pray to God that everyday would be a normal day, even though the word "normal" was not in my dictionary. There was no such thing as a normal day.

Screech! The bus stopped in front of the school. The weatherman was going to be put on punishment for his decisions that morning! I was the last one left on the bus, as usual, and my hands were hurting pretty bad. The entire bus ride, I watched my hands stretch while my right thumb went round and round, like a merry go round. At times, it looked neat because I didn't know hands could do all those cool tricks. I think I broke a few bones during the bus ride.

DING! DING! DING! All of a sudden, I had a brilliant idea! That was another excuse I could add to my great list of how to get out of school early. Someone needs to pay me to write a book. It could be called, "The Book of Excuses for Everyday Situations." I figured that was also called lying, so that was not a good idea since I didn't want anyone to get in trouble, especially me. I thought that Ms. Bracey would be gullible since she was around 134 years old and had been teaching before electricity and cars were invented. Okay, I may not have her age right, but she wears the same dress every day, so she must be at least 133. I'll be nice.

It was starting to become a chore just to resist the eye movements, barks, and now my robotic hands. Inside, I felt like crying because the kids were always staring at me and adults were looking at me like I'm a problem child. Every class I went to, the teachers were prepared to discipline me once I stepped foot into the classroom. What had I done to deserve all of this treatment? Why couldn't I just be normal?

"Bark, Ekk, Ewhh!" I screamed at the beginning of class.

This was in addition to 35 eye blinks, 4 thumb rolls, and 2 finger stretches. OH NO! Not today! Were my body parts competing with each other? I hoped no one noticed.

"Bark, Bark, Squeak!" I screamed, in a real high pitch tone.

"Michael, if I hear one more peep out of you," my teacher Mrs. Bracey said.

Before she finished talking, my face made a grimace (hard to explain what this is -- my eyes rolled up towards the top of my eye lids, my mouth opened real wide, first starting off small) and another bark came out.

This was great, another field trip. Yes, boys and girls, you probably already know where my field trip is. It's the coolest place on earth. "Where is it?" you ask. The field trip was to the principal's office of course; my second home. Before I got into any more trouble, I asked to go to the bathroom. Mrs. Bracey teacher gave me a pass but told me to leave all of my jokes and facial movements in the toilet where they belonged.

I walked down the hallway in tears because once I got to the bathroom, I knew my body would take control and move uncontrollably. Sure enough, I got to the bathroom and let loose. All of the urges I'd been holding in came out. Kids walking by the bathroom heard the echoes of dogs barking and little mice squeaking. If they had opened the bathroom door, they would have seen how much my body was hurting.

Sometimes, to make myself feel better, I convince myself that this stuff is kind of neat. Maybe I can make a living as an entertainer. I could make lots of money by charging students to have me disrupt the class. I could charge $5.00 per student for me to act up during tests. That way, no one would be able to take them. I'm going to be RICH! Wait a minute. That might not work because I'm sure I'll eventually get kicked out of school. It looks like I'll have to go back to Plan B, video games professional.

I went back to class relieved that the war with my body parts was over. The eyes won against the hands, 66 to 59. It was a close match, but the eyes came out with some increased movements near the end of the match. The eyes usually win since they can move faster and easier. My hands fought hard, though. They stretched and my thumb rolled until the last round. Then the eyes knocked them out.

I went back to my seat and saw the students' eyes wandering over at me even though they were supposed to be working. For the rest of the class, my tics were not as bad. They were probably tired from their competition in the bathroom.

The morning went on as usual. By lunch time, I realized that I hadn't gotten kicked out of class. It was a miracle!

# 5

## ROBOTIC HANDS AND VOLLEYBALL, YEAH RIGHT!

L UNCH TIME for most kids is the best time of the day. It's a time when you can hang with your friends and talk about the latest video games, sports teams, and of course, girls. In my school, we have the prettiest girls in the world, but they don't have brains. I say that because if they had a brain, they would all want to marry me when they get older because I'm not that bad looking. Hey, this is my story, so give me a break. Who wouldn't want someone like me around? Oh, did I mention that I'm a pure genius? My grades are not the best, but that's because I'm too smart for the teachers. I don't want to excel too much and make them feel bad. Okay, now for the truth.

Lunchtime for me is no fun. Kids who ask me to sit at their table only want to make fun of me because of my tics. They also think I'm a nerd because I'm short, have a high voice, and do weird things with my body. So I'm the last person they ever want to be friends with. I do have a couple of friends who like me for me. LaRonda is one of my friends. I'll talk about her later, and since I'm the story teller, you'll just have to wait. (I can be a little demanding at times, but you'll live.)

I wish more people would understand me, but since I don't even understand why I do the things I do, it's kind of hard to expect other people to get it. Sometimes, I want to run to a deserted island and live by myself, but that would be no fun since they won't have McDonald's and pizza. They probably don't even have a video game store, so that's a bad idea. But do you get my point? It's just a little hard being me.

The bell sounded so lunch would be over in 5 minutes. All of the kids in my homeroom were excited because we had gym that day. Gym is another challenge. I walked into the gym and sat in the bleachers. My hands were so sore from fighting with them all day. I hadn't told my mom about this new and improved way of having fun.

"Today we're playing volleyball," Mr. Robinson, the PE teacher, said.

"WHAT?" I thought to myself. "How can I play volleyball in this condition?"

I quickly went to my list of excuses to think of

the best one. Okay, it's now time to play America's favorite game, "Guess what excuse Mike is going to use."

### MICHAEL'S LIST OF EXCUSES #3

1. I have a waiver from playing volleyball because I'm allergic to the leather on the ball and the chemicals used to make the stitching.

2. I'm going to the World Olympics for volleyball in 8 years and my contract does not allow me to play outside of my personal training.

3. It's against my religion to play volleyball before 3pm.

Some of these excuses are almost the same as the ones I made up when I had to present my science project. When stretching the truth, you have to make sure you stay consistent. That's why most of the time I don't use my excuses.

"Sir, I can't play volleyball today because I'm allergic to the chemicals that are used to stitch together the leather on the ball," I said.

The kids burst out laughing waiting to see what my teacher was going to say.

"Michael, I'm not going to take your bad behavior today, so please keep quiet," Mr. Robinson said.

Oh man, that didn't work, as if it ever works, but I wanted to at least try.

"Bark, EEek, Ruff!" I screamed.

Oh no, please not this, I thought. I was just told to keep quiet and the urge to bark overtook me.

"Michael, didn't I tell you once to stay quiet? But since you're determined not to listen, please follow me to the hallway."

This was not a new thing since all of my teachers say this when I can't hold in my tics. I stayed in the hallway until class was over. I should be paid to be a hallway policeman as much as I'm out there.

The last class that day was math. We had an oral test. Yes, an oral test, do you believe it? My brother must know the math teacher and set me up to look like an idiot. His time is coming when I'm the President of the United States. He's going to be forced to be nice to all kids my age.

I opened up my math book and my shoulder and right arm began to bother me while my hands moved in a painful way. I felt like moving my arm in a big circle but the urge went away. I guess I was too worried about trying not to scream out. Over the past few months, my behavior, as the teachers would say, had affected my school work and grades. It had been hard to concentrate in class, which made me not understand the work. I just wanted to wake up to make this nightmare go away.

During the exam, I had my barks under control, but my eyes were moving at the speed of sound. Yes, one class that I wasn't going to get kicked out of that day. Out of 5 classes, I had been kicked out of 4, so that is an uh, never mind. I was going to tell you the percentage, but I was too busy twitching when we learned that, sorry. The last bell rang for the day -- a big relief. I had made it through another day of school!

# 6

---

# A NEW DANCE, THE HEAD JERK

THE LAST winter storm passed and spring finally came. That meant longer days and more time to play outside. One Saturday, my mom was downstairs cooking her famous blueberry pancakes and sausage. We were going to the mall later.

"Larry and Michael, the food is ready," mom said.

I tried to beat my brother down the stairs but barely made it to the table without hurting myself. My mom always tells me not to run down the stairs, but I sometimes forget. I was sitting at the table and my brother ignored me like he always does. He does this to make sure he doesn't notice my eyes twitching, fingers rotating, and voice barking.

"Larry, so what are you doing today?" I asked. "I bet you're going to find 100 kids and tell them that if they give you $100, they'll be able to play basketball like Mike."

He continued to ignore me while I talked about my basketball skills and how they are out of this world. I dared him to challenge me but he never takes me up on my offer. When I said "play like Mike," the first person who came to your mind was probably the famous basketball player, but I wasn't talking about him. When people say "I play like Mike," 99.999% of the time they are talking about me. I forgot to tell you that I'm a natural born athlete. That's why my brother is scared to play me in any sport. I think he gave me some medicine to make me tic all the time so I couldn't beat him. Even though I'm only 4' 6" and twitch my eyes at the speed of sound, my jumper is nice.

I can beat him in basketball any day, any time. I have a crossover that not many people can stop. When I play basketball, my tics usually stop. But I have this one crossover called the Tornado...okay I can't tell you what it is because I would have to charge you for basketball lessons. Okay, back to my story. Where was I? Oh yeah, I was talking about my Saturday.

I finished eating all of my pancakes and ran upstairs to brush my teeth before we went to the mall. It can be hard going to the mall because I try my best not to show any of my tics. Have you ever had to sneeze really bad but tried your hardest not to, but then it came out even harder? Well that's how I feel when I have tics. I feel it coming on and try my hardest to stop it, but eventually I can't resist anymore and the tic comes out. That's why going in public places can be really hard.

After I brushed my teeth, I ran downstairs to catch the last part of the morning news........... STOP. That was a joke! HELLO! I'm only a kid and really don't care about the news. No offense to any adults out there, but the news is for you guys.

I'd rather play video games. I just want to make sure that I don't make anyone mad. Oh yeah, I forgot to tell you, if you've made it this far in the book, there are no refunds. Just keep reading and act like you're having fun.

We got to the mall and I started thinking of how embarrassing it would be if I started barking. Sometimes it hurts my feelings when people in public stare at me. I don't understand why people just can't understand that I can't control my tics. Why won't they just leave me alone? Everyone has something unique about them and with me it's just a tic. We walked through the mall and my tics were almost unnoticeable. My mom was happy, my brother was weird, and I was just looking good and happy. I really should be in Hollywood, but I won't have time since I'll be an NBA basketball star by the time I'm 15.

We went from store to store looking for clothes. Of course, my brother went off on his own because at 17 years old it's illegal in his world to be seen in public with his kid brother. He is so weird! I followed my mom and what did I see? A woman's clothing store! Nooooooooooo!!! HELP ME! I hate those stores because they are SO boring. I started getting nervous and tried to think of an excuse to change my mom's mind.

"Okay, Michael," mom said. "Give me one of your reasons why I shouldn't go into this store."

I couldn't figure out what in the world was going on. She was messing me up. I was supposed to start the conversation.

"Mother, whatsoever are you talking about?" I said, trying to sound like an adult.

I tried to sound intelligent to confuse her so she would forget to go in the store. Three-hundred-twenty-two feet away from the entrance and plan A wasn't working, so it was time for plan B. Here are the 3 options I had to choose from.

MICHAEL'S LIST OF EXCUSES #4

1. **Mom, if you go in the store today and buy yourself something, you'll get arrested because it's illegal to buy anything for yourself on a national holiday. You're supposed to spend all of your money on your youngest son.**

2. If you go in the store, you'll turn into a mannequin and have to live in the window forever (same concept as parents telling us that if we keep eating candy, we'll turn into a candy bar).

3. Mom, wait a minute. I really need to go home and study for the rest of the day. We've got to leave right now.

Smart me, I chose #2.

"Mom, you know you're going to turn into a mannequin and have to live in the window forever if you go into that store," I said.

"Wow! Thanks for telling me, Michael, because I always wanted to be a mannequin," my mom said. "Make sure you listen to your brother since he'll have custody of you because your father wants to be a mannequin also."

WHAT? I thought. My brother will have custody of me? He'll send me to a military school and I'll be miserable. Okay, I lost this battle but next time I'm coming back with new material.

We went into my mother's favorite store and I sat down and looked at the wall. My tics were mild, but I started to feel a sensation in my head that I had never felt before. I thought I might be getting a headache. In the next few minutes, while I was sitting in the world's most boring store, my head jerked back and then whipped quickly to the front. I wondered what was going on, if I had just sneezed or something?

"Bang, bang, bang," my head jerked again.

My head shook back and forth a few times and people started noticing me in the store. I heard some people talking about how weird that little boy was acting. Other people were laughing at me like I was invisible. Like I came into the store not knowing they would have tics for sale. That's it. My mom must have bought me a new tic -- a head jerk.

"Why does this have to happen to me?" I thought to myself.

I tried to cover it up before I made a dummy out of myself. I sat there and tried to concentrate to stop my tics. Right after, my hands started moving and my eyes started blinking. Great! This was just great. I was putting on a show in the middle of a store while my mom was in the dressing room. I made sure my tics knew that I did not mean to make them jealous and would promise to get the receipt from my mother to return the head jerk. After I thought this, the finger tics believed me and went away. I was so excited. I figured the others would follow right behind.

"Bark! Bark! Ruff! Ruff!" I screamed.

"What in the world is going on?" a sales lady asked. "Dogs are not allowed in the store."

"Bark! Bark! Eeeeee!"

I was sitting there about to cry because I was so embarrassed. Why couldn't I just be a normal kid without all this extra attention? The sales lady walked up to me and told me to stop barking like a dog. Here would have been a good time to give one of my excuses, but I felt so bad. As people passed me staring and laughing, my mother came out of the dressing room.

"Michael, what is going on here?" mom asked.

"Ma'am, your son is misbehaving," the sales lady said. "He's making sounds and barking like a dog. If he doesn't stop, we'll have to ask you to leave the store."

I sat there afraid that my mom would get mad at me, but the complete opposite thing happened.

"Ms. Madison, how dare you talk about my son in that manner?" my mom said. "My son is perfectly normal and if he wants to bark, well let him bark. This is a free country and we do have freedom of speech. So if you ask us to leave, I'll call the police."

"GET HER! YEAH MOM! That's my mom," I thought.

As we walked out of the store, my eyes were still watery. My mom tried to make me feel better and told me that everything was going to be okay.

"Michael, don't ever worry about what people say about you. You're special in my eyes and I love you."

My heart melted and I moved close to her.

"I love you, too," I told my mom.

For a while, my head jerks went away, but they met me back at the car after we were done shopping. I guess they got tired of walking around in the mall, so they gave me the honor of shopping without them.

# 7

## DETENTION? THE LAST DAY BEFORE SUMMER BREAK? IMPOSSIBLE!

THE SUN was shining through the window, the birds were chirping, and there was the sound of frying bacon sizzling. Oops, that was me chirping and the bacon, yeah right, cereal, maybe. The last day of school before summer break and I was very excited, so excited that my tics were enjoying the freedom of doing whatever they wanted. I left for the school bus and all of my unwelcome friends were with me: Mr. Eye Twitch, Mrs. Finger Tic, Dr. Head Jerk, and oh, don't let me forget my favorite and best friends of all, Mr. & Mrs. Bark. I say they are friends even though they are not real people, but since they are with me all day long, I might as well get used to them.

As normal, I ran down the stairs almost late for the bus. Maybe if my mom would be more responsible and wake me up on time, this wouldn't happen. Did I mention that she wakes me up around 5 times, 2 hours before the bus arrives, every morning to make sure that I'm not late? But my body doesn't believe in waking up on time, but hey, someone has to take the blame and it's not gonna be me.

Running to the bus stop, I saw my brother walking to his bus stop. Just to bother him, I ran up behind his friends and screamed real loud.

"Larry, get your little diseased brother," his friends said.

"I don't know what you're talking about. I don't have a brother," Larry said.

I looked at him and thought, "Oh, the time

will come when you'll need me since I'm going to be a famous basketball player." With all of my skills, he won't even have to drive me around. I will allow him to carry my luggage. Man, I'm a great little brother. I'm very considerate, loving, and giving. Who wouldn't want a job like that? Don't you agree?

I got to the bus stop just in time. I was so excited about it being the last day of school. I could barely control my tics. I had gotten used to kids staring and laughing, and since it was the last day of school, I couldn't care less.

All day long, people were signing each others' yearbooks and exchanging phone numbers. Everyone that is except me! Since everyone thinks I'm weird because of my tics, I don't have a lot of friends. The kids who did sign my book usually cracked a joke just to make fun of me. People called me nerd boy, freak show, monkey, tic-a-zoid, eye blinker, and let's not forget my favorite, Cookiemon the dog. One person who signed my book wrote,

"To Mike: I hope you have a nice summer,

Nerd, and I hope the pound comes to pick you up for barking and trying to bite your neighbor. HA! HA! HA!"

I just couldn't figure out why people had to be so cruel. I do have a few friends who have always treated me like a human. LaRonda wrote this in my book,

"Michael: To my close and dear friend who always makes me laugh. Don't worry about what people say to you because you are cool with me. You will be somebody in life, just you watch. Have a great summer and call me so we can hang out. Your friend, Ronda."

LaRonda and I have been friends since second grade and have had some fun times. I remember last summer; we were walking around the neighborhood in Southfield, Michigan minding our own business. It was a hot, sunny summer day. The neighborhood she lived in was really pretty with trees, flowers, beautiful houses, and big yards. On a normal day, you might see a raccoon, a squirrel, and even an elephant, well maybe not an elephant, but today would be just as weird and different.

"LaRonda, look on the roof. It's a bird," I said.

"Oooohh! Wow! A bird, Michael," LaRonda said. "You've really found something neat today."

As she ignored me and refused to look, I looked in shock at the roof.

"AHHHHHHHHHHHHHH!" LaRonda screamed. "Mike, it's a peacock on Ms. Wiggins' roof!"

We ran up to the house and stared at the peacock on the roof. We were totally shocked. The peacock was walking on the roof trying to get down. The first thing we thought was, "who in the world is going to believe us?" We watched it for about 5 minutes without saying a word. Its tail was beautiful and looked like a fan. We ran back to tell her parents and they called animal control. I don't know how and where that peacock came from, but to this day, it's a funny story that no one believes but LaRonda, me, and her parents.

Okay now back to my last day of class. We went from class to class, waiting to get out for summer vacation. We were almost there and guess what happened? We were sitting in 7$^{th}$ period and Mr. Head Jerk decided to join me for class. My head jerked back and forth to the point where it hurt. I tried to play it off with a sneeze, but my teacher figured out it wasn't. The kids in the class started to stare at me, like always, and I could feel my regular trip to the office coming. So I grabbed my books and thought how great it would be to get in trouble the last period on the last day of school because of something I couldn't control. As I walked out the classroom, the other kids were getting ready to eat the cake and ice cream that our teacher had brought for us, so of course no one was paying me any attention. They couldn't care less about tic boy since cake was way more important.

I walked to the office and the principal was standing right there. I wondered what else could go wrong.

"Mr. Michael, why can't you behave on the last day of school?"

I sat there in silence. No one had believed me the whole year, so what was the point of talking?

I was in the office for 45 minutes and had a lot of time to think. I thought about the past school year. It had started off normal. I went from having friends and being one of the most popular kids in class to being laughed at and disliked because of my behavior. It started with eye twitches and moved to barking and hand movements, then to barking and head jerks. By the end of the year, most of my friends didn't want to be around me anymore. My friends who used to smile at me started laughing in my face. The kids who used to ask me to sit next to them to play games started sitting away from me so that they could talk about me. I wasn't sure why the year had been so rough and how come people had been so mean, but I was glad it was almost over. I sat there and thought about the teachers and the adults at my school. They weren't much help, either. They didn't stop the laughing and thought I needed to be in a special school because my grades dropped a lot and because of what they called, bad behavior. No matter what people were saying, it was summer break and I was going to have fun and get ready for the next school year! I was really glad that I had my mother because she understands me and always puts a smile on my face. I just hope my summer turns out better than my school year did!

# 8

## MR. TYRANNOSAURUS TIC

FOUR WEEKS into my summer vacation and it had been a busy one. Between swimming, playing video games, and skateboarding, what more could a boy ask for? It was Saturday and we were going to stay home. I was planning to go play with my two best friends, Randy and Jay. My father was still asleep and my mom was making breakfast. The smell of the food sneaked up the stairs to my nose to let me know that breakfast was almost done. Now when it comes to food, you don't have to ask me twice. Maybe if my mom would cook like this every morning, and not just every 33 years, I would wake up on time for school. But since both of my parents work, a home-cooked breakfast is a treat.

My mother put the food on the stove and everyone got what they wanted. My brother and I went into the living room to watch cartoons. We sat next to each other with big smiles on our faces, happy it was Saturday and happy to be together. He asked me which cartoon I wanted to watch and then we made plans to play basketball and to spend some time at the mall looking at video games.

SsssTOP! Are you crazy???? If you believed that, you haven't been paying attention at all! Watching cartoons, playing basketball with each other? I feel sick! Come on, let's get real.

After I ate breakfast, I watched cartoons and wished it could be Saturday every day of the week. My favorite tic, the eye twitch, was awake and working. I call it my favorite tic because I can play it off with the allergies excuse. While I was in the living room, my mom was cleaning up the kitchen, getting ready to sew. My mom loves to go upstairs in our patio room and sew while she looks out the window. She hasn't had much time lately, but she had announced to everyone that she was determined to sew, no matter what. Seems like a normal morning, huh? You're right, the morning was pretty normal but then something happened that changed everything. An unexpected visitor came to our house and said a whole bunch of bad words, and we didn't know why. It got pretty ugly in our house. Here's what happend.

The day was almost over, and boy, had it been

fun. Jay, Randy, and I had gone skateboarding for hours. We threw some rocks and went over to our friend Curt's house to play basketball. Of course, I beat them in every game. Okay, I did lose one game of basketball because Randy is 11 years old and must be around 10 feet tall. He's a giant! Since that's ridiculous and isn't fair, that game doesn't count.

The street lights were about to come on and my stomach was screaming "feed me"! I was running back to my house to see what was for dinner, and I noticed the pizza man's car pulling off. I hoped he had dropped some pizza off at my house. I rushed through the door, and what did I smell? I ran through the house looking for the pizza but couldn't find it.

"Mom, where's the pizza?" I asked.

"I'm sorry, Michael, that is for your brother and his friends downstairs," mom said. "Your brother paid for it. You have to ask him for a slice."

WHAT? Ask him for a slice of pizza? This was the same dude who wouldn't admit that I'm a human being just like him. Since I'm one of the smartest kids living with an IQ of around 1000, I decided not to fight that battle. I think IQ stands for Intelligent and Quick. I mean, my eyes twitch quickly, my head jerks quickly, and of course, my basketball crossover is quick, so it makes sense that my IQ is so high. I know you wish you could be me, but don't worry. It's rough being famous and smart.

Dinner was over and my mom went upstairs to start her sewing again. I followed her and lay on the floor to play a game.

"%#$%&*!" I blurted out.

"Michael, what did you just say?" said my mom.

I sat there in shock thinking, what did I just say and why?

"%#$%&*!, Ruf! Bark! %#$%&*!" I said again, this time under my breath.

"Michael, what did you just say? Did you say what I think you said?"

I looked at her and thought to myself, maybe if I tell her she is hearing voices, she'll leave me alone.

"%#$%&*! Mom, %#$%&*!%#$%&*!" I said again.

"Michael, I don't understand where you're learning those words, but they are never to be said while you live in my house. Do you understand?"

"Mom, I can't help it. I don't know what's happening to me."

I have urges to say words that I hear other people say, but I promise I can't help it.

"Larry Sr., come in here at once," mom says.

Now I haven't talked a lot about my father, but he completely ignores my twitches, so I knew she wasn't going to get too far with this conversation.

"Larry Sr., your son is saying bad words under his breath. We have to find out what that's all about."

"Yeah, yeah, yeah, okay," my dad grumbled.

"Michael, don't worry. Everything is going to be okay," mom said.

I sat there trying to resist the urge to scream more words. I ended up running to my room and shutting the door, never wanting to come out again. As if you haven't figured it out yet, the visitor who came to our house was another tic. This was the tic of all tics, the king of all kings, the cookie of all cookies, and the dinosaurs of all dinosaurs. Well, you get my point. Something had to be done. I lay down on my bed and hoped that this would all be over soon. I wondered if I could just wake up out of this nightmare, but I knew I wasn't dreaming.

Since my mother couldn't get anywhere with my father, she called her sister, my Aunt Brenda.

"Brenda, I just don't know what to do anymore," my mom said. "Michael's tics are getting bad. Today, we were in the patio and he started saying bad words under his breath. I asked him about it, and he acted like he didn't know what I was talking about. A few minutes later, he said a few more words and barked and screamed. The scream was so loud, it sounded like a Tyrannosaurus Rex. I asked him again what the problem was and he said he couldn't help it and didn't mean to say it. I told his father, but like normal, Larry Sr. didn't want to hear about it. What do you think"?

"Marilyn, I think he's having trouble with the

talks of divorce between you and Larry Sr.," said my Aunt Bren. "Larry rarely lives there anymore and Michael has to notice it. Maybe you should take him to see a counselor or psychiatrist so he can talk out what he's feeling. I also watched this program on TV about kids with tic disorders. This one kid had some of the same symptoms that Michael has, except his were much worse. It was really interesting. They diagnosed the child with a neurological disorder called Tourette Syndrome. I doubt he has it, but he does have some symptoms."

"Brenda, my son doesn't have any Tourette Syndrome. He's a normal kid and very bright. Please don't even go there."

"Marilyn, I know he is, but he has some of the symptoms. And if he has Tourette Syndrome, that doesn't mean he's not a normal kid. Kids with TS are very intelligent and grow up to be doctors, lawyers, musicians, teachers, and even preachers. All I'm saying is check it out."

"Okay, I'll ask, but I think you're right about it having something to do with my husband not being around as much. I'll schedule an appointment with a counselor at once. Thanks for your help. I'm sorry for snapping at you, but Tourette Syndrome is not what I want in his life. Thanks for talking. Good night. Love you, Brenda."

My mom hung up the phone and quietly came into my room. She noticed me sleeping and kissed me on my forehead.

"Lord, please help my son have a normal life." mom said as a tear dropped down the right side of her face. She turned off the light in hopes that tomorrow the stranger, Mr. Tyrannosaurus Tic, would leave her dear son alone.

# 9

---

# NOW TO MY BIRTHDAY PARTY!

THE FIRST year was rough, but my mother helped me survive. Tomorrow, I turn 13 and go into teenagerhood (don't bother looking it up in the dictionary), and I'm really excited, but a whole lot of things happened last year. I met a psychologist from Mars, went to a brain doctor, and I met someone who changed my whole life. The most exciting part was how I found out that I had a disorder called Tourette Syndrome. I still have lots of stories to tell you about my diagnosis, and since tomorrow is my birthday party, you're going to have to wait to hear all about it in my next book. But until next time, here's a poem I wrote. If you don't like it, just rip this page out of the book. Just kidding, I know you'll like it.

"I have shed many tears but laughed more. I have been talked about by many but more have given me compliments and a smile. I may tic and I may not. Tics wax and wane but I really can't complain. I may bark at you or even chirp at times but it is normal and I don't plan to change. I may twitch my eyes uncontrollably but still see the great things God has in store for me. I may jerk my head, scream out loud, twitch my hands or even shrug my shoulders, but that's just plain old me! Mr. Michael here with TS that is, or as I would say, Tyrannosaurus Tic, that's me!

I can honestly say now that everything is going to be alright, but I didn't always think that. We'll talk later! Good Night.

# APPENDIX

**———**

## ABOUT THE AUTHOR

STEPHEN MICHAEL MCCALL

Stephen Michael McCall was born November 7, 1977 in Cleveland, Ohio. His parents moved him to Detroit, Michigan three years later where he spent the majority of his childhood. McCall started having symptoms of Tourette Syndrome at a young age. His older brother, Larry Cayenne McCall, recollects him making noises when he was only 4 years old, when they had to share a room. Larry thought he was just dreaming, so he never mentioned it to his parents.

At the age of 10, McCall's symptoms started becoming progressively worse. Around this time, a Neurologist diagnosed him with the neurological disorder, Tourette Syndrome. The next couple of years he would be prescribed several medications, from Haldol to Ritalin. Both medications made him very tired and his mother described him as a "Zombie."

Entering high school and adolescence was not easy. Though he knew he had TS, the tics became worse and sometimes uncontrollable. Many of the tics would cause him physical pain. He also had the symptom of TS that is most commonly known and stereotyped by the media, called "Coprolalia." This is a vocal tic where a person screams or says usually obscene or inappropriate words. This was the main reason his mother took him to the neurologist.

Throughout high school, he struggled to

make it as the medication took a toll on him. Stress causes the tics to increase. In his junior year, both of his grandfathers, with whom he was very close, passed away. During this time, McCall was determined to not let TS overtake him. He decided to ask his mother to be taken off medications for good! This is exactly what he did. From the age of 16 to the present, McCall has not taken any medications for his tics but has learned to suppress them.

McCall graduated from High School with a 2.0 grade point average and a sore of 12 on the ACT college entrance exam. Many people told him that he had no future. At first he believed them, but was determined to show everyone that no matter what life brings, if you put your mind to it, you can make something of your life.

He went on to attend a community college and then attended Michigan University for one semester until he decided to join the United States Air Force. From the age of diagnosis, McCall did not believe he had TS, and just thought it was a childhood illness. He learned to adapt and suppress his tics. In 1997, he graduated from Basic Military Training.

Over the next 3 years, McCall would become a highly decorated military veteran. He received many awards from the Airman of the Year to Volunteer of the Year. He has coached almost every sport offered while being stationed at Aviano, Italy. During the Kosovo War, he was under a lot of pressure, working 16 hour days, 6 days a week, attending school, mentoring youth, attending church, and coaching youth sports. This is the first time since high school his TS affected him and became more severe. At one point, he was going to ask the military for a medical discharge after calling his mother and asking her about what TS was all about. For years, McCall had been in denial and did not consider himself to have TS. He decided just to hang in there and trust in the Lord.

At the age of 20, he accepted the Lord into his

life where his whole life would take a turn for the better. Everything started working out for him. He received an Air Force R.O.T.C. scholarship to the world's top-rated aviation school. In 2002, he received his Bachelor's of Science Degree in Aviation Business Administration. He graduated with a cumulative grade point average of a 3.78. He never imagined he would ever accomplish this achievement!

Due to medical reasons of a previous pre-diagnosis of leukemia while attending college, the military medically discharged him due to the chances of cancer being present in future years. From this point, he took a job for the Department of Defense and also became a jurisdictional youth director and a licensed Minister in the Church of the Living God International, Inc.

In 2003, he felt as if he should not hide his life with TS. Because of his love for young people, he decided to start working with the Tourette Syndrome Association (TSA). He founded the first support group in 2004 for the Ft. Walton/ Pensacola counties in the state of Florida. There, a boy named Bradley inspired him to write a book. Bradley wanted to be a preacher and have a secular job when he grew up. He never imagined this was possible since he had TS. Once Bradley and Stephen met, Bradley's dream became achievable. McCall then realized that he had to do more for people with TS and decided to start writing his first book.

Currently, McCall is on the Board of Directors for the Tourette Syndrome Association of Greater Washington Chapter and Co-leader of the Tidewater support group in Virginia Beach, Virginia. He was the featured "Family Portrait" in the Summer of 2007 in TSA's national newsletter. In addition to speaking at schools, spending time with the support group, and having fun, McCall never imagined his life would turn out quite like this. He gives God all the glory, honor, and praise because if it had not been for Him, he would not be where he is today!

**(Tyrannosaurus Tic)**
**Recognizes the**
**TOURETTE SYNDROME ASSOCIATION**

**Thanks for your generous support!!**

# FACTS ABOUT TOURETTE SYNDROME

Answers to Most Commonly Asked Questions

**What is Tourette Syndrome (TS)?**

It is a neurobiological disorder characterized by tics–involuntary, rapid, sudden movements and/or vocal outbursts that occur repeatedly.

**What are the most common symptoms?**

Symptoms change periodically in number, frequency, type and severity–even disappearing for weeks or months at a time. Commonly, **motor tics** may be eye blinking, head jerking, shoulder shrugging and facial grimacing. **Vocally**: throat clearing, sniffing and tongue clicking.

## What is the cause of the syndrome?

No definite cause has yet been established, but considerable evidence points to abnormal metabolism of at least one brain chemical called dopamine.

## How many people are affected?

As TS often goes undiagnosed, no exact figure can be given. But authoritative estimates indicate that some 200,000 people in the United States are known to have the disorder. All races and ethnic groups are affected.

## Is it inherited?

Genetic studies indicate that TS is inherited as a dominant gene, with about 50% chance of passing the gene from parent to child. Sons are three to four times more likely than daughters to exhibit TS.

## Is obscene language (coprolalia) a typical symptom of TS?

Definitely not. The fact is that cursing, uttering obscenities, and ethnic slurs are manifested by fewer than 15% of people with TS. Too often, however, the media seize upon this symptom for its sensational effect.

## Do outbursts of personal, ethnic and other slurs by people with TS reflect their true feelings?

On the contrary. The very rare use of ethnic slurs stems from an uncontrollable urge to voice the forbidden even when it is directly opposite to the actual beliefs of the person voicing it.

## How is TS diagnosed?

Diagnosis is made by observing symptoms and evaluating the history of their onset. No blood analysis, X-ray or other type of medical test can identify this condition. The TS symptoms usually emerge between 5 and 18 years of age.

## How is it treated?

While there is no cure, medications are available to help control TS symptoms. They range from atypical neuroleptics, to neuroleptics, to anti-hyperactive drugs, to anti-depressants. Individuals react differently to the various medications, and frequently it takes some time until the right substance and dosage for each person is achieved. Almost all of the medications prescribed for TS treatment do not have a specific FDA indication for the disorder.

## Is there a remission?

Many people with TS get better, not worse, as they mature. In a small minority of cases symptoms remit completely in adulthood.

## Do children with TS have special educational needs?

As a group, children with TS have the same IQ range as the population at large. But problems in dealing with tics, often combined with attention deficits and other learning difficulties, may call for special education assistance. Examples of teaching strategies include the following: technical help, such as tape recorders, typewriters or computers to assist reading and writing and access to tutoring in a resource room. Under federal law, an identification ("child with a disability") under the *other health impaired* category may entitle the student to an Individual Education Plan.

## What future faces people with TS?

In general, people with TS lead productive lives and can anticipate a normal life span. Despite problems of varying severity, many reach high levels of achievement and number in their ranks as surgeons, psychiatrists, teachers, executives, professional musicians and athletes.

## For more information please contact:

*Tourette Syndrome Association*
*42-40 Bell Boulevard, Suite 205*
*Bayside, New York 11361*
*(718) 224-2999 fax: (718) 279-9596*
*http://tsa-usa.org*
*email: ts@tsa-usa.org*

**(Tyrannosaurus Tic Sponsor)**
**Recognizes the**
**MARYLAND AUTISM ASSOCIATION**

**Thanks for your generous support!!**

# FACTS ABOUT AUTISIM

**What are Autism Spectrum Disorders?**

Autism Spectrum Disorders (ASDs) are a group of developmental disabilities caused by a problem with the brain. There is usually nothing about how a person with an ASD looks that sets him/her apart from other people, but they may communicate, interact, behave, and learn in ways that are different from most people. The thinking and learning abilities of people with ASDs can vary – from gifted to severely challenged.

**What are the most common symptoms?**

People with ASDs may have problems with social, emotional, and communication skills. They might repeat certain behaviors and might not want to change in their daily activities. Many people with ASDs also have different ways of learning, paying attention, or reacting to particular situations.

**What is the cause of the syndrome?**

There is no known single cause for ASDs. It is generally accepted that ASDs are caused by abnormalities in brain structure or function, since brain scans show differences in the shape and structure of the brain in autistic versus non-autistic children. Researchers are investigating a number of theories, including the link between heredity, genetics and medical problems.

**How many people are affected?**

A 2007 Centers for Disease Control report found that 1 in 150 children in America are affected by ASDs.

## How ASDs diagnosed?

There are no medical tests for diagnosing ASDs. People with ASDs have some degree of impairment in social interaction, social communication and imagination. To be diagnosed as having an ASD, a child must be observed over time by professionals skilled in determining communication, behavioral and developmental levels.

## How are ASDs treated?

Right now, the main research-based treatment for ASDs is intensive structured teaching of skills, often called behavioral intervention. It is very important to begin this intervention as early as possible in order to help the child affected by ASDs reach his or her full potential. Acting early can make a real difference!

**For More information please contact:**

*Autism Society of America*
*7910 Woodmont Avenue, Suite 300,*
*Bethesda, Maryland 20814-3067*

1.800.3AUTISM    www.autism-society.org

# HELPFUL RESOURCES/WEBSITES

National Tourette Syndrome Association, Inc.
(718) 224-2999
http://tsa-usa.org

Tourette Syndrome Association of Greater
Washington (TSAGW)
www.tsagw.org

Tourette Syndrome Association of Florida
www.tsa-fl.org

Tyrannosaurus Tic Series Official Site
www.tyrannotic.com or www.stephenmccall.com

# MICHAEL'S TOP TEN EXCUSES

1. I have allergies even though it is not allergy season.
2. I'm doing a science project on goldfish that have blinking problems.
3. I'm practicing for the World Olympics, "The Eye Blinking Contest."
4. I'm not blinking. What are you talking about?
5. I'm practicing for a play called, "All dogs bark in Detroit."
6. That was not a bark, that was a scream so what is the problem?
7. I have a waiver from playing volleyball because I'm allergic to the leather on the ball and the chemicals used to make the stitching.
8. I can't stop moving my hands because they are turning into robotic hands.

9. Why are you asking me questions? I need to talk to my lawyer before I answer your question of, "Why are you shrugging your shoulders and blinking your eyes?"

10. That noise, what noise? Have you heard of the bird calling competition? Well yes, I am the world champion for birds and dogs.

# TS HELPFUL TIPS & MICHAEL'S FAMOUS PHRASES

1. Life is filled with many challenges and hurdles, but TS helps you overcome them.
2. Tourette's is like Water, you can't live without it!
3. Good Night and don't let the TS Tics bite
4. Some people have blonde hair, others black; some people are tall and some are short; some people like driving and some like flying; Some have TS and some don't; Who cares which one you are because we are all human and made equal
5. Tics are like holding in a sneeze and eventually it has to come out so when it comes out, just say God Bless You versus staring at me.
6. What time is it? It is TS time!